Fairy Tales

from around the world

by

TEYA EVANS

Table of Contents

Introduction

Do you read bedtime stories for your child? Don't modern heroes seems too boring to you? Try to plunge into the fairy tale world filled with ancient, magical creatures: elves, fairies, mermaids, dragons...

This fairy tale storybook is dedicated to ancient folktales from around the world. Many of them are lost, but some have still managed to reach our era.

We travel, together, all around the world. We sink into the old tales that speak of magic we still don't fully understand. We look for answers, but — perhaps more importantly — we look for questions: for that spirit that makes us stare in reverent wonder at the world around us.

Our ancestors told of these magical creatures from generation to generation. And it is surprising how similar their habits are. Perhaps by reading some of the tales from another continent, you will find that her characters are exactly the same as in your grandmother's tales. Who knows?

And then, perhaps, you tell this story to your child.

And you will pass it on to the next generation.

And now...

Pretend you're sitting by a fire, listening to a wise, wizened storyteller begin to talk...

The Loneliest Place

New Zealand

If you have ever sailed the seas around the land of the Maori people, you might have noticed you were not alone. Those who dare look into the water that their ship or canoe traverses will, perhaps, see a great silhouette, dark and confusing. It is a marakihau.

What, you ask? A marakihau is an ancient being, a guardian of sorts. They have a head and torso just as human as you and I, but, instead of legs, they have an extremely long and powerful tail. They eat fish, men, canoes, sharks — anything that falls within the scope of their searching, tubular tongues. But fear often overruns knowledge, and few now remember how the first marakihau came to be, and why.

Long ago, in the land of Whakatane, there ruled a fair and well-respected chief called Te Tahi o te rangi. He protected his people from war and from hunger, making sure they were always safe from enemies and had enough food to feed their families.

However, some were envious of his glory and might. They decided to trick and betray him. In the council house of the clan, in the midst of an assembly, the rivals captured him and, sailing to a deserted island, left Te Tahi o te rangi to die.

Thirsty days and hungry nights passed. At last, when he realised no one could come to save him, the chief gathered all of his remaining strength.

With power and valour he called forth the monsters of the deep water — the sort of sea monsters no one ever wants to look upon. Despite this, what he sought was not vengeance: it was the safe passage. He wanted to go back to his people, to keep protecting them and defending them against the bad men who had tried to murder him.

And the sea monsters did the bidding of the good and valiant chief. They took him and restored him to his land and to his people. Seeing this, his enemies escaped. When the people asked Te Tahi o te rangi why he did not seek revenge, he wisely replied, 'They will be punished by their own shame.'

Te Tahi o te rangi ruled his people fairly for many years. After his death, they took his body to the water and, there, something marvelous happened.

He breathed again, and moved again, and his legs turned into the tail and fins of the sea creatures. He and his descendants still roam the Southern Seas, defending the unprotected and guiding the lost. Just as the monsters of the deep had helped him in life, now Te Tahi o te rangi would help his beloved people stay safe, forevermore.

The Queen of the Huldufolk

Iceland

In cold Iceland high in the mountains, there was a farmstead. In it lived an unmarried kindly farmer, with all his relatives and helpers. He was prosperous — not least because of his thrifty housekeeper, Hildur. Quiet and unassuming, Hildur took care of the house - overseeing the cooks and servants, and making sure everything ran smoothly. She kept to herself, but was invaluable and well-liked by everyone. She was also beautiful, although she hid it under rough clothing.

The only problem in the farmstead was finding a herdsman. Over the last eight years, the farmer had hired eight different herdsmen. Not one lasted more than one year. Without fail, on Christmas morning, they would be found mysteriously dead in their beds. Hildur, the only one who didn't go to the Christmas service because of her duties, never saw anything. There never were signs of violence, but no one in the region wanted to herd for the farmer any longer.

Now without a herdsman, there could be no flock as the land was dangerous. Resigned, the farmer had decided to take his chances and leave the sheep alone, when a stranger turned up. He was as tall and strong a man as the farmer had ever seen! When he offered to take on the job, the farmer refused. 'It'd be a sad thing to let a strapping lad such as yourself die! Find a job elsewhere.' But the stranger insisted, saying he didn't care for death and ghostly legends. Eventually, the farmer relented.

The sheep had a herdsman again. He worked hard and everyone liked him. On Christmas Eve as they went to the church service, they were sad and thought the man would not see morning. He, however, was as cheerful as ever and went to bed, although he guessed it'd be smart to stay awake. Just in case.

Sure enough, after a while, the herdsman felt an unnatural fatigue stealing over his limbs. He fought against it: no one was going to surprise him. When the door creaked open, he pretended to be asleep. The footsteps came closer. Even in the darkness, he recognised the figure: it was Hildur, the housekeeper.

Stunned, he realised she was putting something cold in his mouth — a bridle! He couldn't move of his own will but remained awake when she led him out of the house, mounted his back like a horse and took off into the chilly night sky.

They flew over snowy meadows, creeks and mountains until arriving at a gigantic, dark precipice that opened like a cavernous mouth. Hildur commanded him to land next to it, and she tied the bridle to a rocky outcrop. Then, leaving him there, she leapt into the abyss.

By now, the bewildered herdsman knew the quiet Hildur was no human. This could only be the work of a magical creature. Always brave, he refused to simply die of exposure and, with a huge effort, managed to slip off the bridle. After stretching his exhausted muscles, he looked into the chasm. Darkness. With a surprising presence of mind, he breathed in deeply and jumped after Hildur.

As he fell, he realised the darkness had changed into light and colours. At the bottom he didn't crash but landed softly on sweet-smelling grass. While outside it was midwinter, here there were flowers everywhere! And, in the middle of a meadow by a golden palace, a crowd of beautiful people were cheering, singing and hugging

Hildur. A kingly man approached her and kissed her cheek like a husband does. 'The hidden people, the dangerous huldufolk!', the herdsman thought, and paled. He decided to stay hidden.

The celebration went on, and, at one point a fairy child took one of Hildur's golden rings and dropped it while playing with it. The herdsman reached out and he pocketed it. After some time, Hildur and the King became sad. He begged her to stay with him. All the fair folk in the ravine kingdom begged her. 'I cannot,' she said, 'You know I cannot'. The herdsman saw her look at an old, bitter-looking woman in a corner. 'Mother, please, lift the curse' pleaded the King, but the old woman turned away.

With tears, Hildur parted from the King. Thanks to the magic ring, the herdsman made it up the cliffside before her and slipped the bridle back over his head as if nothing had happened. Crying, Hildur rode him back to the farmstead. He felt his heart and limbs would explode from the speed and, sure enough, Hildur left him for dead on his bed.

He was sick for many days, but (thanks to the fairy ring) didn't die. On the New Year, to everyone's surprise he made it to the hall. Looking into the astonished face of his master, he told him of Hildur's deeds and of everything that had happened.

'Lies!' she said 'I'm innocent, you can't prove this

slander!' Holding up her magic ring, he asked her to swear it wasn't hers. In response, she burst into laughter: it seemed to everyone she became taller, more beautiful and lighter. 'Bless you, Herdsman. You have set me free.'

She told them her story: she, a lowly peasant among the Huldufolk, had fallen in love with their King and he with her, to the bitter disapproval of his mother. When they were handfasted, she cursed her to live among humans — to serve them! — and to only come back once a year on Christmas Eve, at the cost of a human life. If she didn't go back, she'd die. If the humans found her out, she'd die for the crimes she'd been forced to commit.

'But you changed everything! As a human who went to our realm — and can prove it — you have lifted the curse. You will be blessed all the days of your life.' At that she disappeared back into the Hidden Realm, to be with her love and her people.

The farmer who had treated her well became even more prosperous. And the brave, gallant Herdsman became a great chieftain and was rich and joyful every day of his life.

An Onion and a Lindworm

Scandinavia

Once upon a time, in a remote corner of the North, there lived a king and a queen, much beloved by their subjects, but childless. Despite a good marriage and their strong wish to have a son or daughter, they had almost lost all faith in being able to conceive.

On a particularly lonely winter day, the Queen decided she could not live this way anymore. She wanted — needed— a baby or she would die of grief. Distraught, she went off into the dark and perilous forest, though what she wanted, she knew not. She realised she had lost her way but, before she could be afraid, she saw an old Crone, looking at her from the shadows— with kindness.

'Dear Queen,' the old woman said, 'I see that you are set upon this course. So you will not die, I will show you how to have a child. You must do exactly as I bid and not disobey me, or terrible things will happen.' The Crone gave the Queen one huge, red onion and told her to peel it perfectly before eating.

Doubtful but filled with new hope, the Queen rushed home and, in her hurry to see if the Crone's words were true, forgot to peel the red onion before eating it. 'No matter,' she thought, 'if I have a child, everything else is trifling.' And, true enough, nine months later, the joyous couple announced the birth of a child.

The whole kingdom rejoiced greatly, but the sovereigns were troubled— they had an unsettling secret: the child that had been born was no child at all! It was covered in red and black scales, had fiery serpent eyes, two sharp claws, and a long tail! Fearful for the life of their infant, they built a secure, secluded chamber for him to grow up in. They brought him cattle and he would eat it raw. He grew and grew into a horrible monster, and it was now clear— the Queen, because of her haste and disobedience, had given birth to a *lindworm*!

The lindworm infant became a child, then a youth, and was, always, alone and friendless. The people were, still, blissfully unaware of the dreadful, dragonish nature of their Prince. So, when the King and Queen, uncomfortable but determined to keep the traditions, announced their son was seeking a wife, the nobles and important families were delighted to send their daughters as potential brides. When the maidens arrived in the castle, dressed in all their finery and looking as beautiful as ever, the King would take them to meet the Prince, who also said he was keen to be married.

However, once they entered the isolated bedchamber of the Lindworm Prince, he snatched them up, one by one, and devoured them whole. This happened, again and again, and the families had no news of their daughters. No one wanted to send a maiden to the castle anymore, and the Lindworm Prince threatened to escape and eat them all by force. Desperate, the royal couple sent far and wide for a new, brave bride. No one came.

When all hope was lost and the Prince was about to set out on a course of devastation, there came a piece of news. A young woman, a beautiful but poor shepherdess, had come. She told the worried Queen to be still— she had spoken to an old woman who, pleased with her bravery in keeping the sheep, had told her what to do.

She was wearing seven dresses— her whole dowry— all at once and was carrying a bowl of milk.

So she went into the frightful chamber and when she saw the Lindworm, she didn't flinch. He snarled that she should take off her dress so he could eat her without trouble, and his eyes were fiery slits. 'On one condition,' she said, 'That when I take off one dress, you take off one of yours.' 'Deal,' the Lindworm Prince agreed, wild with hunger. The shepherdess took off the first layer of clothing and, forced by his own word to comply, he shed one layer of skin, just like a serpent.

'Off. Another one,' he said. But he was already weaker from the shedding. As the maiden took off the dresses she wore, one by one, the dragon sloughed off one layer of skin after another. With each dress she took off, the shepherdess was unharmed, but the lindworm grew weaker: it isn't easy to take off your skin. When the maiden was down to the last dress, the Prince no longer thought of eating her: he was in excruciating pain, even as he agonizingly discarded his last layer of dragon skin. The girl watched, surprised, as there, in a dead faint, lay a bleeding Prince— a human prince!— on the chamber's floor.

She rushed to his side and, with the milk the Crone had told her to bring, she bathed the wounds of the former Lindworm. He, having shed off all the layers of scaly dragon skin (just like an onion), was cured. The King and Queen rejoiced. The two young people loved each other, and the Prince had, finally, found someone who challenged and bettered him to become, instead of a monstrous Lindworm, a good man.

Menana of the Waterfall

North America (Ottowa)

Stories are like the water: beautiful, nourishing, always new, always flowing. Once a seasoned warrior was kneeling next to a waterfall, getting ready to drink, when he saw someone unexpected: a maiden in the water! Her hair was long and strewn about her, filled with waves and river flowers. Her arms and chest were covered in scales; her legs were two fish tails. 'If you let me live and go in peace,' she said, seeing the warrior's spear, 'I'll tell you a story very old, but never heard by humans before.'

After the warrior had agreed to the deal (not that he would have harmed the maiden anyway, but you should never turn down a good story), she began...

Long ago, in that same land, there had lived a daughter of an important medicine man. After her father died she was sorrowful, and wanted nothing to do with the world anymore. She searched her heart and, at last, asked the Great Spirit to turn her into something that could roam the water in the sky. She wanted to explore, she wanted to see the majesty of the stars.

Moved by her request, the Great Spirit granted her petition and she was free to traverse the heavens as she pleased. Long she travelled, much she saw, but at last she grew tired and wished for the earth again.

When she returned, she found that everything had changed and she would forever remain in the shape of a mermaid: neither a human nor a swimming thing, but between. She was adopted by the Spirits of the Flood and was, eventually, allowed to become human again. The only condition was that she had to find a human who would love her.

One day a man went down to fetch water and found her, and they talked. Moved by what she had told him, he decided to take her to the land and love her as if she were his own daughter. He called her Mennana.

Time passed and, being loved by a human father, the maiden lost, one by one, her gills and her scales. She became so beautiful to human eyes that the very son of the main chief fell in love with her. When he secretly told her of his deep love, she cried tears of joy. She realised that meant that she had finally gained a human soul! She was just like him, and their love was possible!

However, their fate was not to be so simple, nor so fortunate. The chief looked down on the mermaid girl and he publicly said, 'No son of mine will marry a Spirit of the Flood, one of those who has done so much harm to my people.' To the horror and great grief of Mennana, her human father, and Piskaret, the chief's own son, he banished her.

Menanna was brokenhearted. She had nowhere to go, as she was too human now to return to the Spirits of the Flood. Taking pity on her again, the Great Spirit saw her plight and told her to go and live at the waterfall. She should be safe there.

She obeyed with a heavy heart, and thought her love, Piskaret, was lost to her. The Spirits of the Flood came to her and consoled her. Seeing one of their own (for they still thought of her as such) in such a sad state, they waged war on those who had hurt her so: the chief and his tribe.

The Spirits of the Flood waited until all the tribe was on their canoes, sailing downstream to their hunting grounds. Then they attacked. Only a few people escaped: those of them who had been kind to the Flood Spirit Girl.

Among them was Piskaret who, shielded by the arms of his love Mennana, survived. The malicious members of the tribe that had been defeated were turned into eagles, never to be allowed to rest.

Mennana and Piskaret lived by the waterfall, together with the good people of the tribe and the Spirits of the Flood, for many years. They loved each other greatly and, from their happy union came I, the mermaid who is telling you this story.

The warrior smiled, stood up and thanked the mermaid for the tale. His mood was lighter and his heart was cleansed from all sorrow — this is what water and its inhabitants always do for us.

Aminata and the Tokoloshe

South Africa

Have you not wondered why wasps have such thin waists? It wasn't always that way - only after Aminata's story.

Aminata was a lovely girl, but a little disobedient. She loved her plants and flowers more than duties and chores. So, when the villagers had to burn the fields (like they did every year) and the King ordered everyone to stay home, Aminata didn't pay attention and went out to water her flowers.

Now she knew that when the fields burned, the evil elven Tokoloshes that lived under the earth could come up to hurt people. But Aminata thought they were just an old wives' tales - and besides, a Tokoloshe wouldn't hurt someone as pretty as her.

Aminata was planting new flowers and making little holes when none other than a Tokoloshe cropped up with a mean grin. 'You'll be my wife, little girl. And I'll make sure you obey me better than you obey your elders.' Aminata of course wanted none of this nonsense, so she ran away.

She soon became tired, fell down and began to sob. A nearby wasp asked, 'Beautiful Aminata, why do you cry?' 'The Tokoloshe wants to take me away to be his wife,' she wailed. The wasp, always smart, devised a plan. It told Aminata to sit still and not move; not even when the Tokoloshe was close.

The girl was, for the first time, quick to do as asked. She sat frozen under the blazing sun and when the Tokoloshe approached, she didn't move. When he was almost on her, the wily wasp flew down and swallowed the Tokoloshe whole!

'Quick!' it said, 'Grab a thread and bind my waist!' Aminata did as she was told and the Tokoloshe was forever trapped inside the wasp.

From that day Aminata paid more attention to the stories her elders told her, and the wasp has the thinnest waist in the world.

The Great Master and the Rainbow

Benin

Long before man walked on the earth and fished in the streams, before even the oldest of the animal bones lived and breathed, there was Nothing. No planets, no starry night sky, no rocks underfoot— nothing.

In the great Void, there was only the primeval serpent Damballa, a *loa* (god) of immeasurable power. He was the root from which all the worlds sprouted. How did this happen? Well, Damballa saw that there was nothing around him and did not want it to be so. But there was nothing he could use to create the world— only…

Damballa considered his own body, the only thing that existed. He was strong, and big, and awesome (if anyone had been able to see him, they would've agreed): he could do this!

Using the power and incredible length of the 7,000 coils of his body, Damballa curled and stretched and took shape. He danced a serpentine, dragonish dance until everything was the way he wanted. In this way, the Great Dragon Master created the whole cosmos: the stars suspended in the sky, the uncountable planets, the highs and lows of every valley and hill on Earth, the bones of every mountain. By shedding his skin, he completed his work— his shining, flowing scales became the water we drink, present in every spring, ocean, and waterfall.

After this great task, he was tired and felt lonely. Though he had created the world by himself, he couldn't take care of it on his own. But, when the waters he had made rose from the ground and fell again as the rain, he saw he was no longer truly alone— he saw *her*. Ayida-Hwedo, the green dragon serpent that is also the rainbow. And she was the beauty.

Damballa, happier even than when he'd created the brilliant gems in the core of the earth, took her as a wife. He tasked her, his beloved, with holding up the skies and filling the waters of the earth with the whisper of amazement.

Through the ages, the love of Damballa and Ayida-Hwedo, the two dragons that are the Masters of the world, has endured. In every child that is born, we can see the fruits of their love, for mankind sprang out of it. And in every corner of the world we see and the air we breathe, the two Great Dragons continue their primeval dance of creation and entrancement.

The Paddlers

North America (Passamaquoddy)

Once, long ago, in a land where the cold meets the sea, there lived a man, a woman, and their two young daughters. They were happy together, and spent their days singing, playing, walking by the lake near their house, and tending the land in peace. The father and mother loved each other as well as both their daughters, and they loved them equally as much.

There was only one thing that was not right: the lake. On fair days it seemed inviting enough but, when the weather grew darker, it sat ominously in the background. It was big enough for there to be crashing waves on nights of storms, and the sorts of hidden currents that like to take people away from the shore and down to unknown fates. It was strange. It was eerie.

The man and his wife did not like to think about the lake. Daily, they told their young daughters, 'You must not swim in the lake: it is too dangerous', they said, 'Please. We don't want you to drown. We love you. We don't know what could happen.'

And, yet, summer after summer, the growing girls did not pay any attention to their parents' sound order. Instead, they liked to swim in the dark water. At first they stayed close to the shoreline but, with every passing year, they ventured further and further out. They felt guilty, yes, but they said to each other, 'There is no way for our parents to find out, so it will not hurt them.' And, just like that, they were swimming in the deepest parts of the water as if they had been born to it.

That summer the two girls went to the lake tirelessly, day after day after day. Where before they had felt guilty about disobeying their parents' order, now they thought the day's swim was sweeter because of it. Still, they made sure no one saw them. In a deep place in their hearts, though they would not show it to each other, an opaque fear lurked.

The parents, at first, did not suspect a thing! They thought their daughters were walking by the forest's eaves, or fishing, or feeding the cattle. But, one clear evening, as the two girls took off the day's clothing to go to bed, the mother caught a glimpse of something out of place in one of the shirts. A bit of reed? No, it couldn't be! That would mean the girls were disobeying them, it would mean they were in danger!

A cold dread settled in her bones and chilled her. Danger from what? She didn't know, but she was not going to wait to find out the hard way. The very next morning, the mother thought that they would follow their daughters. They would see what they were up to.

On that fateful day the little sisters acted as usual, had their usual breakfast and, as usual, said goodbye to their worried parents with a kiss. They headed out. 'The air feels different today,' the eldest said. 'I wonder what that means,' replied the youngest. But a light breeze came, and the lake was already in sight, so they decided to ponder it later.

After laying their clothes on the grassy bank, the girls waded, barefoot, into the water. They did not know that it was the last time their toes would touch the earth.

From far away, the parents looked on in horror. Their daughters were getting in that dreadful lake! As soon as they could react, they ran towards the water.

Alas, the two girls were already too far in: they were swimming, and laughing, and playing. However, all their merriment turned to fear when they looked towards the bank and saw, among the reeds, the stricken faces of their parents.

As if waking from a dream, they immediately turned. The dread in the expressions of their father and mother gave them pause, and their own hearts reflected back at them the fear of the water that they had thought long gone. Hearts now pounding fast, they hurriedly tried to kick their feet beneath the murky surface of the lake and then…

To their horror, they discovered that no matter how hard they tried, they could not do that. With ever-increasing disquiet, they raised their legs to the surface.

Legs, however, were nowhere to be found. All the girls and their now weeping parents could see were two long, scaly, twisted fish tails that started at the waist and ended, instead of human feet, in translucent salmon fins.

The old man and his wife cried out, 'Let us take your clothes and cover your tails.' When the girls tried to talk, they found themselves singing in response, 'Do not touch them, leave them there!'.

'What will we do? What will we do?' continued the distraught elders. The newly-turned mermaids sang, melodiously, back, 'It is our fault, that much is true, but it will not be worse for you! When you go to your canoe, we shall paddle instead of you!'

And so, from that day onwards, whenever the father and mother went fishing or sailing to visit relatives, the two mermaid daughters helped them. They had more fish than ever before, became very wealthy, and were never parted. In this way, they turned something that seemed most terrible into a blessing.

The Gifts of the Little People

United States of America (Iroquois)

There was a couple who had a little son. They loved each other and their son deeply and fiercely, but life in those days was unpredictable and hard. One day, the boy's mother looked at him very seriously and said, 'My son, I feel we might not be with you long, but we love you very much. This is what I want you to know: if you walk with a heart full of good, you don't need to be afraid.'

As the mother predicted, a sickness took both her and her husband shortly after and the boy went to live with his aunt and uncle, who hated him. He never had enough to eat, he did all the hard work and he only wore tattered rags. Making fun of him, they called him 'Dirty Clothes'.

Since he had to fend for himself, Dirty Clothes became a mightily skilled hunter. But even though his marksmanship was unerring and his bravery steadfast, he had a kind heart. He never killed animals or hurt living creatures unless he absolutely needed to. Dirty Clothes often hunted by the river, near the rocky cliffside.

This was further than any others in the village dared to go as it was close to where the Little People, the much-feared Jo-Ge-Oh, beat their dread drums in the dead of night. But Dirty Clothes, even with a changed name, remembered his mother's kindly words: if you walk with a heart full of good, you don't need to be afraid.

One day while hunting in the forest he heard small, odd voices. They were discussing how to best shoot at a squirrel that was nearby. They just couldn't seem to hit it! Taking pity on them Dirty Clothes hunted the animal for them and, approaching the voices, he found two tiny people — the Jo-Ge-Oh! Scared but curious, he handed the squirrel to them. 'Have this, little brothers,' he said, 'and these other animals I hunted are yours too. You won't go hungry.'

The Jo-Ge-Oh were ecstatic — they'd never seen a human so close before, and certainly none that was so kind. They were grateful, too, and invited him to their village with a smile. When Dirty Clothes got into a (tiny) canoe with them, he was astounded to see that his body shrunk down to fit. And he was even more surprised when the vessel started flying!

The wondrous, soaring canoe glided into a cave in the cliffside, where they gave him food and clothes. There was much singing and celebration, and Dirty Clothes felt happy for the first time in a long, long while.

The wanted to thank him for his goodness by teaching him their secret ways and wisdom, and he stayed with them for a short time. Dirty Clothes learned how to tell the birds apart by their sounds, how to grow nourishing squash and corn and how to find precious strawberries in the summer grass. And, most importantly, the Jo-Ge-Oh made him learn a new dance to teach his people. Thanks to this dance, the Little People would become friends of the humans and they would dance together and exchange gifts.

After four days of learning and dancing, two of the Jo-Ge-Oh hunters led the boy back to the human village. When he turned back to say goodbye, they were gone. The village came out to receive him, but he realised they thought him a stranger!

'Don't you know me?' he said to his aunt and uncle, 'I am Dirty Clothes!' 'It can't be' they replied, and showed him his reflection: he was a grown man with the most handsome features, the strongest arms and the most elegant clothing.

Dirty Clothes realised his time among the Jo-Ge-Oh had changed him. The gifts of the Little People had been bountiful and generous. He told his story and, eventually, they came to believe this authoritative young warrior.

The people learned a better way of life, and they learned the Dark Dance that Dirty Clothes taught them. So every night when the village gathers to dance around the fire, they can hear the Jo-Ge-Oh dancing along in the distance in newfound harmony with their human friends.

Short-Tailed Old Li

China

In the poorest of the South Eastern provinces, a farmer's wife (whose name was Li) was in labor. Her husband was out working in the fields, as they were very poor and could not afford to be idle, not even for something as important as birth. The land was dry, desertic, and miserable.

It was hard. There was no midwife to help the poor woman push— she had to guess and do everything by herself. But she loved this baby and was determined to do right, whatever it cost. She labored from sunrise until sundown and, with the last, terrible push, was exhausted. She felt the baby crawling up to her breast— odd. Her tired thoughts couldn't focus on why that was strange though. As she felt the baby start to suckle— sharp teeth? —, she dozed off.

That was how the husband, returning from the field, found them: his wife, lying spent on the bed. And an odd, serpentine shape attached at her breast. He was horrified — that ugly thing could not be his baby!

Full of dread, fear for his wife's life, and sinister thoughts, the farmer grabbed a spade that was in the corner and swung it at the little serpent. A screech. A severed tail. The baby creature opened wings it didn't know it and escaped, with a shower of sparks, out of the window— just as the mother opened her eyes and tried, in vain, to catch her son.

Many sad moons passed between the now lonely and estranged couple. As the middle of May came around, with the anniversary of that terrible day, something odd began to happen. Rains came. Monsoons. Awe-striking thunderstorms that fertilised the land, making it flourish and give fruit like it never had before. And, on the thirteenth of the month, he came.

It was their son! Only, now, he was full grown: a

huge, majestic, kindly dragon. He had flown to the far north and, divine as he was (even with a short tail), had become the god of a rich river. Now, he said, he had come back to visit his mother, the one who loved him despite his appearance.

And, though he disregarded his father, he went back to visit her— bringing fortune, fertility, and good luck—every year. He still did, even after her death, to honour her memory. He had become Short-Tail Old Li (just as she was also Li), the dragon that brings rain and abundance, every lunar year, because of a mother's love.

For the Cause of a Bridge

Thailand

Hanuman, a king of great power and renown, wanted to build a bridge over a calm, flowing stretch of water. He needed to get to the other side without pause, as he needed to rescue Sita, the wife of his dear friend, who had been kidnapped. And, because he couldn't very well build enough boats for his endless army, he needed to build that bridge.

The problem was that, try as they might, the workers could not lay the foundations of the pass without them crumbling. Time after time they laid stone upon stone, and, time after time, what they built came crashing down. It was a disaster. Sita was still with her captors, in grave peril, and time was slipping away from between Hanuman's fingers like the sand of the bank he stood on, looking on the proceedings with increasing desperation.

When he could no longer stand the delay, the King instructed his soldiers to discover what was wrong with the riverbed. They needed this bridge, and it could no longer wait. Many men went down into the water, but none returned. Something was very, very bad. Day after day, the same thing happened: he would order a number of soldiers (accomplished swimmers, all of them) to dive into the water. Not one of them came out. Hanuman's numbers were now dwindling as fast as his time.

At last, the King decided he would go himself. He needed to see. And, as he knew, it was the honorable thing to do. To the despair of his remaining soldiers, the King took off his royal robes and adornments and jumped into the water. It was a long time until they saw him again.

Hanuman swam easily. Strangely enough, he found this water was very strange: he could breathe in it without drowning! When he got close enough to where the bridge's foundations were being laid down, he saw something unexpected: many maidens — or, at least, maidens from the waist up — were carrying away the stones and casting them aside! It was all their fault!

After watching them for some time, he found their leader: she was a marvelous creature with radiant, pearly skin, long hair like the softest reed, and a tail like a magical fish. He would have admired her, if she had not been directing the rest of the water maidens to ruin his precious bridge.

He had to stop her. However, when he tried to approach her, the mermaid saw him and, quick as lightning, shifted aside and kept ordering the destruction of the stones. They danced like this for a while but, as the hours went by, Hanuman found himself more and more captivated by the creature. He no longer cared about bridges, or kidnapped wives. He started to woo her and, to his immense surprise and joy, she responded in kind.

Realising his intentions had changed, Suvannamaccha (for such was her given name) approached the King and introduced herself. 'I am the Queen of the Sea,' she said, 'and you are invading my domain.' Hanuman finally understood but, no longer caring, replied, 'Suvannamaccha, O courteous Queen, forgive me! I no longer wish to trouble you — but, rather, to go to your palace and there dwell with you in peace.'

Smiling, the Mermaid Queen guided the way. When they arrived, fascinated by each other's presence, in the Great Hall, the King wondered at the view: among many joyful mermaids were all of his lost men!

There, in the Sea Queen's palace, they feasted long. There were songs, and tales, and a strange, watery dance. King Hanuman and Queen Suvannamaccha had, as it happens, fallen deeply in love.

However, after a season of happiness, a shadow of doubt entered the King's mind: he had left his people. He had left his kingdom unprotected, and his mission incomplete. His beloved Queen saw this and, not without sorrow, said, 'My beloved, I see you are unhappy. I have grown to love you and would loathe to part, but I cannot keep you from what your heart wishes to do.' And, because of their great love, Hanuman was able to build the bridge over the Sea Queen's domain and depart to fulfill his mission with sorrow in his heart.

In the end, he and his soldiers arrived at the far land where Sita was, still, a prisoner. With many great deeds of arms they rescued her and brought her back to her own land and people. Many poets sang great songs about the valour and the glory of King Hanuman.

The king himself, though, could not find rest. Parting from his beloved had broken his heart and, though he still cared about his people greatly, he found he could no longer live among them for long. His heart longed for the Sea.

Finally, after many years, it was done. The King left the Kingdom to his only son and, travelling far, reached the shore. It is said that there, where water meets the land, King Hanuman and Queen Suvannamaccha met again and, like the noblest spirits among us, chose Love. What became of their fate after that, we do not know.

The Birch Lady

Czech Republic

Betushka was always singing. She was the only daughter of a poor widow and had to work all day to help her mother. She wore old dresses and spent her days spinning the wool and tending the goats in the meadow. Even so, Betushka was always happy. She loved to sing and dance but had to work too much.

One day the girl took the goats to a pasture by the riverside, where there was a cluster of birch trees to shield her from the summer sun. She spun and spun the yarn but, when she lifted her eyes, she could see the birches swaying — dancing? — in the breeze. Betushka tried to focus. Dancing meant she couldn't finish her work before nighttime.

At midday, she heard a voice that sounded like water. 'I've seen you dance. Come dance with me'. She turned and, standing there, was a beautiful lady clad all in silver. She smiled at Betushka and the girl couldn't say no. She danced with the Lady, hand in hand. Birds and silver leaves twirled around them. A melodious tune rose from the earth. A moment later the Lady parted from her, smiled, and was gone.

Betushka rubbed her eyes. The sun was dangerously low, and she hadn't finished her work. Her mother would be so cross! She didn't sing as she walked the goats home, so her mother asked if she was ill. 'No,' she said, but felt guilty and mentioned nothing about the Lady.

The next day she thought, 'Today I'll double the work so my poor mother will be happy.' At midday, the Lady was there again. 'I cannot dance today', exclaimed Betushka, 'I must make my mother happy.' The Lady replied, 'You have a good heart. Do not worry about it. Come dance!'

And dance they did. Out of the corner of her eye, Betushka saw the spindle twirl along with them. Before leaving, the Lady said 'Wind the spindle and complain not!' It was full! She didn't tell her mother anything, but the old woman eyed her suspiciously.

On the third day Betushka returned to the birches and, at midday, the Lady appeared, took her by the waist and spun her around in the most joyful dance. When the sun went down the Lady took Betushka's bag, whispered something, and said 'Don't look at it until you're home. Dance, wind and complain not'. On her way back, the girl's curiosity overpowered her and she looked inside the bag. There was no spindle, only birch leaves!

She started to cry and cried even harder when she got home and her mother asked angrily, 'What evil spirit spun for you yesterday?' Betushka confessed everything.

In wonder, her mother exclaimed 'It was a Wood Fairy! They drive boys mad but give marvellous presents to little girls like you! What's inside the bag?' When they looked, instead of leaves there were countless precious jewels and gold!

After that day, Betushka never had to graze goats or wear old dresses. They used the Lady's gold to buy a new, better farm and lived happily ever after. Betushka didn't see the Lady again, but she went to the birch wood to dance and smiled, knowing that her friend was there.

Two Horses and one *Zmej*

Serbia

The youngest son of an Emperor fell in love with an enchanted princess that, every night, stole a magic fruit from his father's garden. Their love was tested when his older brothers found out and cut off a strand of the maiden's hair. After giving the youngest prince a longing look, she flew away in the form of a peahen.

As love always prevails, he found her after a long and arduous journey and, of course, they were married with much joy and became Emperor and Empress of a wide realm. But the castle where they lived their love was ancient and held many dark secrets. 'Don't go into the twelfth cellar, not for anything in the world,' she warned.

But one day, after the Empress had just set out on a journey, the young Emperor (of course!) went down to the cellar and a casket asked him for water. One, two, three times. The man thought it was strange, but it was rude to refuse water. Suddenly, after the third time, the casket exploded!

Out of the million fragments came crawling a *zmej*, an age-old, evil, winged dragon, made stronger and more fierce by its long forced confinement. It was wicked, incredibly powerful, and would not stop until it got revenge on its captors (who had put it in the casket as punishment for its wrongdoings). The Emperor understood this and knew that, even as the *zmej* flew off, he had little time to rescue his wife.

He found her before the dragon did. Together, they rode upon one horse, without knowing where they went—only escaping. They could feel the *zmej* chasing them but it had assumed human form and was following hard on another horse. But though human in form, the *zmej* was dragonish in weight, and the poor mare it rode on was very, very tired.

'I can't go on!' it said to the *zmej*, 'You weigh too

much, you won't let me eat or drink— I will die of exhaustion!' The mare was of the mind that whatever revenge the *zmej* wanted against the Empress and her husband was, certainly, not as important as the life of the mare herself. But she was forced to gallop onwards.

Because of the magical power of dragonkind, the *zmej* and its steed reached the Empress and Emperor, who were riding on their own tired— but very wise— horse. This horse had belonged to a witch and, having learned everything there is to know about dragons and other monsters, he knew exactly what to say to the *zmej*'s poor mare. 'He's killing you, don't you see?' the Emperor's horse exclaimed, 'It's a *zmej*, of course he doesn't care if you live or die— all their kind are so big and majestic that they only think of their own power and vengeance plots. Our lives are nothing to them!'

The mare, already panting hard, saw the truth in the words of the Emperor's horse and, stopping with a jolt, threw the human body of the *zmej* down, breaking its neck and ending its wicked life. The Emperor and Empress returned to the castle and lived happily ever after. And thus, the wise and humble defeated the evil and powerful, and love reigned overall.

Mami Wata

West Africa

No one truly knows who Mami Wata is. There are those who tell stories of great fear: of surviving tempestuous sea journeys during which they heard the most beautiful songs luring them into the deadly water. But there are also others who jump to her defense: she has given them wealth, power, beauty, wishes they had never dreamt of fulfilling.

Mami Wata is like the water that never rests: ever flowing, shifting, majestic, and deep. On the coast where the Sun sets over the sea, she is loved as well as feared. On starry nights, she sits with her court of mermaid handmaidens in the shallow waves and waits for brave souls to come out. She combs her hair with a golden comb and gazes, in a golden mirror, into her own eyes. Her elegant fishtail glistens in the moonlight.

Visiting Mami Wata is a perilous journey. You might be made rich and powerful beyond belief, turned into someone respected by everyone and eternally lovely, but you might also be lured away by her divine voice, far into the water, never to be seen again.

Once, a wise young woman decided to go look for Mami Wata on the darkened beach. She knew it was a dangerous thing to do, but she wanted to bring wealth and beauty to her family and village so that no one would be sad or poor again. She was aware she could die, but her heart told her to be brave, for only the brave accomplish great things.

Setting her mind on the task and her heart on helping herself and her loved ones, she approached the shoreline. Scales and glowing skin. She was there.

The woman waded, determined, into the saltwater — deeper, deeper, towards the divine mermaid who was now looking at her with an unreadable smirk. She saw the comb in Mami Wata's hand. And, in it, a radiant strand of hair. Suddenly, the girl lost her balance: an undertow! She was being carried away!

Terrified but still clear-headed, the young woman saw only the comb. As she reached the side of the beautiful water spirit, she reached out and, swiftly, held fast. She had the hair strand! Everything stopped.

Disoriented, the woman looked up. There, Mami Wata was looking down at her. She was smiling now, and spoke with a voice that was at once a wild tempest and a clear brook, 'You are brave. That is more beautiful than any greed. If you give me back my hair, I will make you lovely as one of my handmaidens as well as very, very rich.'

The young woman marveled at this, and gave back Mami Wata's hair at once. The sea goddess smiled one last time and, just as a wild ocean calms down in an instant, disappeared from sight.

When the young woman, all dripping from her adventure, returned to her farmstead, she saw that everything she owned had been greatly increased! Her image in the mirror was, truly, like the loveliest mermaid. And she was forever lucky, rich, and free: she had won the favour of Mami Wata.

The Poor Boy and Kijimuna

Japan

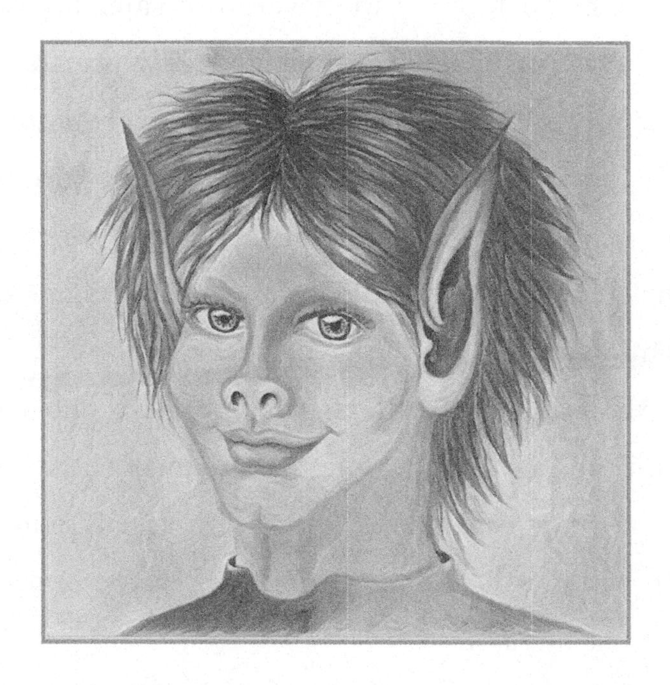

In the wildland of Japan there lived a tree sprite named Kijimuna. The Kijimuna are elves with flaming red hair and very large heads. They look like children and, true to form, they befriend human children. Unfortunately, they often behave like children themselves — they can be wily and mercurial.

One day a poor boy from a fishing village was sitting on a rock that overlooked the ocean, and lamenting being so poor. He used to have friends but, as they were much richer, they stopped playing with him. In his sadness, he didn't see the approaching Kijimuna until it spoke. 'Why are you crying? I can be your friend'.

The poor boy was filled with joy and, when the Kijimuna made him swear never to disappoint him, he thought nothing of it and wholeheartedly promised. The little elf proceeded to teach him the secret Kijimuna arts of fishing and gave him all the fish he caught (after eating the eyes!). The boy sold all the fish and received great wealth. They promised to always meet at the same hour.

This went on until the boy was very rich — even richer than his rich village friends! But, one day, he decided that he was not going to go to meet the Kijimuna. Instead he'd stay home playing with the human boys. Though he knew he'd done wrong, he enjoyed himself and thought nothing of it.

The Kijimuna waited and waited, but the boy didn't arrive. 'He has broken his promise,' the Kijimuna realised and became very angry. So when the boy went home after playing, he couldn't recognise his home: there was nothing there! No beautiful mansion, no riches — only a poor hut. He'd used the Kijimuna for riches and betrayed his friendship, so he was right back where he started. And there he remained.

Y Ddraig Goch

Wales

In earlier times, Great Britain was a lot more forests than in the later days. The cover of trees was so thick on the land that a squirrel could have hopped from the South to the North without ever touching the ground. And, in the vast thickness of the woods, many things lived that are, now, unknown.

One such thing was dragons. No one will ever know the shapes, temperaments and sizes of the many dragons that once lived in the Welsh wildlands, since no one was ever brave enough to go meet them. However, the tale of the most famous among them will always be remembered.

Llud, the Briton King of Wales, was worried. He knew that his land wasn't really his, but belonged to itself and to the many creatures that inhabited it. But he considered himself responsible for the safety and happiness of everyone in it. And, lately, a dragon had been causing problems. It was big, winged, red and, while that in itself was harmless, its screams were making the cattle die and the plants dry out in the ground. Why? It seemed like it was being attacked by a white dragon, come from over the sea, that wanted to kill it.

The King was at a loss. A human, even if he was a King, should not get mixed up in dragon battles. But he had to do something, so he went to his brother Llefelys, who was known to be extremely wise, for advice.

'Brother,' Llefelys replied, 'here is what you must do to protect your people. Follow my instructions faithfully'. He told Llud to dig a well in the very heart of his kingdom — one large enough to hold both beasts inside—, to fill it with mead (dragons are, as everyone knows, great lovers of mead), and to act fast. Llefelys gave Llud a magic cloth. The King nodded and promised to do as he was ordered.

After digging and filling the well with mead, Llud waited out of sight. Soon enough, the two endlessly fighting dragons appeared, biting and tearing at each other. When they saw the mead, however, they folded their wings and rushed to drink. They drank so much that they became quite drowsy and, having emptied the well, they forgot all about fighting and laid down to sleep.

Llud and his men sprang into action! They covered the beasts with the magic cloth and a large slab of white stone, so they would continue to sleep and their devastation would be over.

Someone, though, made a prophecy: there would be a chief who would inadvertently build a castle on top of the dragons' resting place and set them free again. That day, Y Ddraig Goch (the Red Dragon) would kill the white one and set his British land free, once and for all.

Kapsirko and the Vodianoi

Ukraine

Kapsirko was a wily peasant who served a strict lord. Life was hard, but they always worked hard and pulled through. During an especially harsh winter, however, everyone — old men and elderly women, tired mothers and their newborns — was unbearably cold. They asked Kapsirko, who had a reputation as a very cunning man, to devise a plan. And, moved by their plight, our hero did something risky: he stole firewood from their lord, who was away.

Everything was well until the nobleman returned. Noticing the stolen wood he guessed it was Kapsirko, his tricksy servant. However, he couldn't prove it. Because of that, the Lord gave the peasant a choice: he could admit that he did it and be banished to the frozen wastes of Siberia, or accomplish an impossible task that would prove his innocence. Not having any other choice, Kapsirko accepted.

The master said, 'You must steal my wife from my house, and I must not be able to find her. Then, I will know that you are innocent.' That could be done. Kapsirko had an idea.

In the Lord's land there were many nooks and crannies no-one knew but him, as he was exceedingly curious. That is how he knew that, at the bottom of the lake, there lived a vodianoi.

Now, these are dangerous creatures: mean, hairy, and old, with a penchant for mischief, vodianois dwell in water - shapeshifting between an ancient man and an enormous fish. They silently ambush distracted passersby and pull them into the water to eat them. But Kapsirko knew he was more astute than the most ancient of vodianois.

So, at night, he slunk into the Lord's house and carried away the sleeping Lady. Down, down, down to the lake. He waited for the water creature to come out and, when he did, proposed, 'If you fill my hat with gold, I will sell this lady to you'. The vodianoi, being always hungry, accepted.

It must be said that Kapsirko, cunning as he was, had made a hole in the hat so that, when the sprite poured gold into it, it all fell into Kapsirko's pocket until he was satisfied.

A week passed. The Lord called the peasant and said, 'It seems you are innocent; now, give me my wife.' Kapsirko went pale. He did not know how to get her back. He hoped the vodianoi hadn't eaten her already. Anguished, he thought and thought. A plan took shape.

Kapsirko carried an unassuming rope down to the water and hid it among the grasses of the bank. 'Vodianoi!' he called, 'I challenge you: whoever whistles loud enough to make the other fall into the water, wins the Lady!' 'Ha!' thought the vodianoi, 'He shall fall into the water and I will eat them both', and so he came out and accepted the game.

As the challenged the vodianoi went first: he whistled so loudly that Kapsirko nearly toppled over. Having held his ground, it was his turn— but he knew he was nowhere near as powerful. That is why, when he let out a long whistle, he also pulled on the hidden rope. What a ruse! The vodianoi fell headfirst into the water and was compelled to give back the Lady who, returning (dripping!) to her husband, cleared Kapsirko of all guilt.

Our astute hero, as we know, had stashed away a good share of gold, taken from the vodianoi through guile. However, he did not keep it selfishly. Rather he shared it with all his friends and relatives, and no one was cold during the winter ever again.

The Multitude of Bow-Legged Ones

New Zealand (Maori)

The forests of the island were dark, abundant and full of the strangest forms of life. Its deep coves and recesses hid many secrets, and each clan (or hapu) had its own wise men and women who knew those secrets and how to honour them best.

Each of these experts had their own jobs to do, and they had to do them in harmony with the spirits of the forest lest terrible things befell them and the clan. But, sometimes, the youngest and most arrogant among the villagers could be a bit hasty and offend the protectors of the forest.

Rata was one such young fellow. He had big plans to build a majestic canoe and travel on his own around the island to get power and riches. He did not think that he should tell his relatives, nor delay his important plans to recite the traditional incantations before felling the tree that was to become his new canoe.

Hack, hack, hack. Rata brought the great trunk down. Suddenly, a dark cloud enveloped him. It was made of tiny beings: wasps, beetles, mosquitoes and — most importantly — a strange type of creature that chilled his very bones. It was the Hakuturi, the guardians of the forest! Surely they would punish him terribly.

However, the fairies didn't immediately attack. What he heard next was a rousing chorus of shrill voices that accused him in perfect unison: 'How dare you, little man, disrespect an Old Forest God such as this? This was not your right!' Cowering in absolute shame, Rata said he was sorry.

Relenting, the Hakuturi went to work. The multitude of bow-legged ones lifted the majestic old tree and placed it back upright, knitting back together the wounds Rata's axe had caused. Then they said to the remorseful man, 'We see you respect the forest now. We shall not harm you. Instead, we will make you a great gift. All you need to do is return to your village, tell your relatives everything and come back here tomorrow.'

Sorry to have been so selfish and disrespectful towards his family and the trees, Rata did as he was asked to.

The next day when he returned with his relatives, he found the most wondrous canoe anyone had ever seen. Its body had been made by the Hakuturi, the forest fairies themselves! The bow and the stern — the proudest parts of the ship — were carved by the nifty spiders. It was more than Rata had ever dreamed of, and he knew who to be thankful to. He honoured the mysterious forest as long as he lived.

The Naga Dowry

Cambodia

Once, the land at the southernmost tip of Orient was a large and powerful empire. The people were proud, hard-working and imaginative. They built many great temples out of stone and, though they are, today, covered by moss and silence, their ancient glory remains. The secret of the Cambodian people, they said, was in who their ancestors were— or, rather, *what* they were.

Before any humans came to live in the region, this was the kingdom of the Nagas. Varied in shape and size, the Nagas are all powerful beyond our imagination: they are magical, almost divine beings. Magical shapeshifters, they can alternate between their human and their dragon bodies at will, and, as Kings and Queens of the Underworld, they rule over all its precious gems and treasures. In many occasions, they have ruled over humans, befriended them, or— as in this case— even married them

One night, an Indian Brahmin prince named Preah Thong had a dream. In it, an aged sage commanded him to sail East, towards the Sun, and to act with faith, honesty, and love. Now, the lands in the East were not uninhabited, but ruled by an old Naga King called Sdech Neak, benevolent but wily, as Nagas are wont to be.

Preah Thong set sail and, with hope in his heart, arrived at a small island. It was as far East as he could make it on his own, and he was tired. Leaning against a tree, he slept for three full days and, waking by the light of a midnight moon, saw the most wondrous sight. It was the loveliest maiden he had ever seen! Her movements were like the water, and her skin seemed to reflect the moonlight with an enchanting glow of its own. Unable to help himself, he approached her and, when their eyes met, they fell inevitably, irrevocably in love.

'O human,' she said, 'This is strange! Never have I seen a man as handsome and kindly as you, and yet I am a Naga, Neang Neak, the daughter of Sdech Neak, the King. We are not supposed to marry.' But, as their hearts were already joined, she decided to face her father in his Underwater Kingdom. Neang Neak commanded the prince to hold onto her silver clothing, and they descended swiftly, through wave and coral reef.

The Dragon King, surprisingly, said nothing about the oddness of the match and married them: it was willed by fate. But, after some time in the Underwater Kingdom of the Nagas, Preah Thong got very sick. However ill and pale he got, though, he refused to leave his Naga bride, because he loved her more than his own life.

Seeing this, the Naga King smiled a shrewd grin—his daughter's suitor had passed the test. Of course, a human prince couldn't live underwater! Now wholeheartedly approving of the match, the Naga King gave his daughter, the Dragon Princess Neang Neak, a rich dowry: he used his magic powers to suck all the water from around the island on which the couple met and let it be joined to the mainland.

This land, imbued with the gifts of the Nagas, became abundant, fertile, and prosperous. Of the union of the prince Preah Thong and Neang Neak, the Naga princess, came the inhabitants of the empire of Cambodia, whose descendants are alive today, perpetually embodying the union of the human and the magical.

Marina of the Wave

Ireland

On the green coasts of the Emerald Isle there are many tales of water, its beauty and its unknown, fascinating dangers. Old fishermen and sailors are particularly fond of one story — they take every chance to warn and amaze young listeners with their accounts of the merrow folk.

Who are these creatures? Well, from the waist up merrow maidens look like the most beautiful of humans — so beautiful, in fact, that the unwary have been known to stare at them for hours and hours, until the tide carries them and they are never seen again. From the waist down, though, they are all the slinkiest, slimiest, scaly fish in the ocean — and, certainly, the wiliest and most temperamental. It is said that merrow men are, however, of a frightful appearance, causing the maidens to kidnap human men. Few humans come out victorious from encounters with them. Those who do rely upon, as it is known, on iron — it is poison to the merrow.

One such person was named Luty of Kerry. He was a good lad who worked hard at his farm near the coast, and also enjoyed fishing for himself, his fiancée, and his sick neighbours. However, Luty didn't have grandparents, or any older folk who could warn him about merrows, so what came to pass was, sooner or later, bound to happen.

On a warm summer afternoon Luty was knee-deep in the mild waves, looking for straying fish to spear, when he caught a glimpse of something — someone? — unexpected... He shielded his eyes from the sun and, sure enough, there, in the water, there was the loveliest maiden he had ever seen. Her hair was dripping gold; her eyes were the unknowable grey of the ocean. And yet Luty felt a pang of fear — there was something wild in those pupils. When surprise started to leave him, he saw it, poking from underneath the water in scaly, shimmering coils: a fish's tail.

Luty could hardly speak, but, when the maiden smiled a toothy grin at him and said 'I am Marina... Marina of the Wave,' he managed to bow like a good gentleman should before a lady. Pleased, she continued. 'Since you have here found me, take me down to deeper water and I will grant you three wishes. Choose well, son of man.'

Of course, Luty carried her to where the waves grew bigger and, after much reflection, said, 'Lady Marina, there is nothing for me that I want — only this: to be able to break spells, to make spirits do good things for the world, and for these two powers to pass to my sons and their sons as well'.

The merrow-maid looked at him with awe: never had she met a more generous, good-spirited man. Luty had asked for good things not for himself, but for the happiness of the world! So, as he went to shake her hand and depart, she gripped his arm with a steely hold and said, 'I wish for you to stay with me. I can make you rich and happy in my home beneath the sea'.

Luty hesitated. She was beautiful; the promise, tempting. But he could not abandon his fiancée or those villagers who depended on him. And, besides, there was something eerie about Marina. Something that set off bells of warning inside his chest. So, quite reluctantly, he reached behind his back and pulled out a thin iron knife.

Immediately, Marina let him go, terrified. 'That is well, son of man. But I will return to claim you in nine years' time. Do not forget,' she exclaimed before diving, swiftly, beneath the waves.

But human memories are short. Luty soon married his beloved and, when their first son was born with the dew of Spring, he put all thoughts of the merrow-maid out of his heart. Years went by, and children came. Luty was happy and well-respected in the village.

It came to pass, after nine years, that Luty was fishing in the shallow water. His eldest son was with him, watching. Suddenly a shapely, pale arm came, like lightning, out of the water and held the hero by the leg. Now he remembered her. Luty fought, staring at his son with wide eyes, but the arm was too strong. His lips seemed to be sealed, and he could not use his powers to order the merrow to let him go. He was going to drown.

As the water reached his neck, he heard it. His son. A spell was woven of good things and protection, wrapping around him and lifting him up, out of Marina's reach. Forever foiled, she swam away to be happy with her own people. He was saved. And, as we know, it was because he asked for wishes generously, keeping the good of humankind at heart.

The Tale of Curupira

Brazil (Tupí)

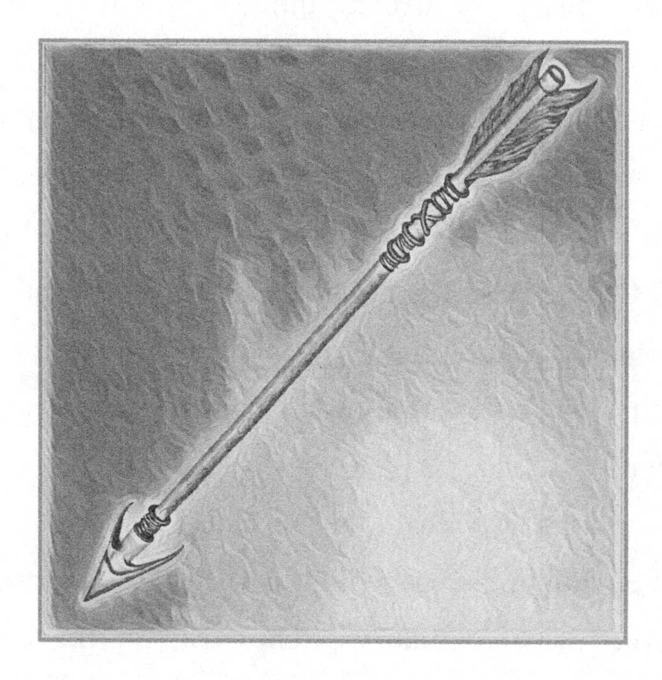

What is very strong, bald and three feet tall, with feet turned backwards? What is hairy all over with blue-green teeth and pointed ears?

In the deep jungle, with their feet thudding along hidden paths while they are keeping watch on every creature live the Curupira. They can take care of you too but, if you hurt trees or pick and hunt more than you need to eat they will come after you and deceive you, and you will be forever lost.

There was, in a small village surrounded by rainforest, a hunter called Joao. He had a wife who was very meddlesome and demanding, so he had to go out and hunt a lot. Late one evening he was trudging along an overgrown footpath, already quite disoriented, when he heard quiet wood-tapping noises: a Curupira was near.

Joao followed the sounds and, indeed, he came face to face with a Curupira — it was the strangest creature, all body hair and bent feet. He'd never seen anything like it. The Curupira smiled a slow smile at Joao and said 'I know you can't find your way back, Hunter, and I can help you. But, first, you need to feed me — I've never been hungrier.'

Now Joao was afraid but, as he really needed help to get out of the jungle, he sat down with the Curupira next to a tree. It was almost pitch dark, so the creature couldn't see the monkey Joao had caught and was carrying.

'I'm hungry. Give me your hand to eat.' So Joao cut off the monkey's hand and passed it to the Curupira, who devoured it in the blink of an eye. 'Still hungry. Give me your other hand to eat.' The hunter used his knife to hack off the monkey's other hand and gave it to the Curupira, who relished the taste. At last, the creature said, 'I need some more food. Give me your heart.' Alarmed, Joao cut out the monkey's heart and the Curupira ate that too.

Then it said 'I am content. Ask for whatever you want.' Joao, who was not silly and thought the forest guardian would eat him when he realised the trick, replied 'I am hungry too — give me your heart so that I can eat and be content!' Bound to his word the Curupira opened his own chest with Joao's knife, handed him his heart and — seemingly —dropped dead. When morning came, Joao found his way out of the forest.

Hunter that he was, he could not stop thinking about all the good things he could make from the Curupira's precious teeth. He went back to get them but as he pulled out the knife that was still coming out of the creature's chest, it woke up.

'My friend,' the Curupira said, 'I thank you for coming back for me after all this time. As you show your heart is good, I will give you a gift: an enchanted arrow. It will bring you good luck in every hunting journey. All you have to do is keep it in a secret place and not show it to anyone — not even to your wife.' Joao thanked him, promised to obey and left in high spirits. After that day he was the best hunter in the jungle and everyone envied him.

His wife, however, was not happy — she wanted, needed, to know what her husband's secret was. She kept nagging and pestering him about it until he was so annoyed that he forgot the Curupira's warning and showed her the enchanted arrow.

When he next went out hunting, he notched his

magical arrow (as always) and aimed at the grazing tapir (as always). But, when the arrow left the bow, something unusual happened: it turned into a flying serpent and disappeared in the vegetation. This was because Joao the hunter couldn't keep a secret and betrayed his promise to the guardian of the forest, the Curupira.

For a Bag of Rice

Japan

Fujiwara no Hidesato was the young son of a famous warrior who lived in a town by a river. No one had crossed the river in living memory, because, on the bridge that crossed the wild water, there lay a most fearsome dragon.

It was serpentine, long, coiled on itself, and huge. It had been sleeping for two thousand years and, in all that time, no one had dared walked across the water. However, Hidesato longed to go to the other side, as he was a most curious young man. His bravery and desire for learning run deeper than whatever fear a dragon could cause, so he began to walk across the bridge.

Despite being careful, Hidesato stepped on one of the creature's whiskers and, with a flurry of scales, the immense being rose, twirled, roared... and then sank into the river, leaving the boy intact.

Too stunned for words, he did not move until a maiden, dripping with silver droplets and bathed in light, rose from the water. Standing before the flabbergasted Hidesato, she said with a laughing voice, 'Brave man, at last, you've come! I have been waiting for one such as you for many a year. I have a perilous enemy, you see, the venomous Ōmukade centipede, and I can only trust to be my champion someone who is not afraid to face me.' Awed, Hidesato agreed to face Ōmukade on her behalf and, donning his family arms, set out.

Being our hero, he (of course) defeated the terrible monster on top of Mount Mikami. He fired three fiery arrows directly into the centipede's bright eyes and vanquished it forever, keeping his word to the Dragon Maiden.

When he came back, bathed in glory and a little worse for wear, she was waiting for him at the bridge. 'You have saved me!' she exclaimed and, filled with gratitude, dived with him into the river. Hidesato was surprised: he could breathe underwater! Looking into the Dragon Maiden's eyes, he understood it was her magic that protected him, just as he had protected her.

Swimming in dragon form, she took him to the Underwater Castle and, once there, she changed back into human form and regaled him with the most delicious food and music Hidesato had ever heard.

As a reward for his exemplary faithfulness, virtue, and courage, she gave the young warrior five gifts: a temple bell, dragon-forged armor, a magic sword, a piece of silk that would last forever, and a bag of rice that would never run out, no matter how many people ate from it nor for how long.

Hidesato returned to the surface world carrying these precious treasures and the blessing from the Dragon Maiden. He went on to become a great warrior and a prosperous, beloved chieftain. In honour of his courageous adventure and the generosity he showed with his gifts, everyone called him 'My Lord Bag of Rice'.

The Fiddle Player

Scandinavia

There was, deep in the cold and damp forest, the most beautiful, magical waterfall. Its magical qualities were not the sort of 'turning water into gold', or of the very sought-after type with miraculous healing properties. Not at all. This particular waterfall was magical because, in it, lived someone very rare: a mighty Fossegrim.

Who? A Fossegrim! Though you might find it hard to meet one these days, they used to be much friendlier at the time of our tale. They are water-spirits, sometimes human in appearance, sometimes indistinguishable from very large, toothy fish. Unlike most water-dwellers, however, the Fossegrim are not ill-disposed towards humans, and can even have relationships with them after their own fashion. The most special thing about the Fossegrim, though, is their peerless knack for playing the fiddle.

This particular Fossegrim was especially good, and played twelve different melodies that bewitched the senses and the mind. The thirteenth melody, however, he reserved for when he was alone with the trees and the stones. Why? He wasn't a malicious being, and he knew that whoever (or whatever) heard that tune would never be able to stop dancing. This is why the plants, animals, and stones around his waterfall always seemed to be shifting, restless as the soul of the Fossegrim.

Every now and then, a villager would brave the darkness of the forest and go seek him out. They wanted to play the fiddle just like the Fossegrim. They wanted to make the world dance. And, of course, the wily spirit would teach them— but at a price. The would-be student had to traverse the forest carrying a bound white goat as an offering, and then throw it into the water without regret. Why? Well, a Fossegrim has to eat, too; and fish gets tiresome after a century or two.

Sometimes the villager would offer the best and fattest goat he possessed, without a hint of sadness. This meant he understood just how precious the gift of the

Fossegrim was: it would turn the generous spirit of the villager into a fiddle player that would enchant any listener— someone the world would adore. However, at other times a villager thought they could get away with gifting a slim animal — after all, it was only a spirit, right?

Because of the wholehearted generosity of the first kind of student, the Fossegrim would seize their hand and mercilessly run the fingertips over the strings of his own fiddle until they all bled. But, if presented with the second kind, the Fossegrim would smile a smile cold and clear as the water of his fall and play his thirteenth melody. After that the person would be able to tune a fiddle to perfection, but never to play it. And they would never cease dancing along to a tune heard by no-one else.

Fayiz and The Peri Wife

Iran

Fayiz was a handsome young man with a loving wife and two children. He lived in the rocky Persian mountains and spent his days playing the flute as he watched over his flock. He was a marvellous flautist, as well as honest and true of heart.

But one day as he played, he felt a strange presence nearby. It was the most beautiful maiden he'd ever seen! The moment their eyes met, an entrancing love was born. Fayiz forgot everything about goats, family and home. When the maiden said 'Come and live with me,' he followed without question. He'd go anywhere with her.

When they arrived at the maiden's house, far up on

the mountain, Fayiz looked around and was dazzled. Never had he seen more riches, more servants or more beauty. As he looked at the maiden, he saw her clearly: she wasn't human. That only made him love her more, and they became husband and wife.

When they were married, they vowed to always be faithful to each other and true. The maiden said 'I wed thee under the condition that you betray me not: this way, you'll always be happy. If you are faithless, as humans are wont to do, you will never see me again and will always be troubled.' And she added, 'If you betray what you know, that I am of Peri stock, I will be gone forever with the sons that we shall have.'

Many years passed. The couple had two Peri sons, loved each other deeply and enjoyed every day together. But, one day, Fayiz longed to see his human sons again. She exclaimed, 'You will regret this choice, human man!' but let him go, repeating the warning to not betray her secret. She recited an incantation.

In a heartbeat he was, again, on the rock where he had played the flute. He hurried back to his town to see his sons. But although he didn't know it, his Peri wife was there watching over him.

He found his family — though he was the same, they had aged and grown up. They demanded to know where he'd been all those years, and why he'd abandoned them.

After days of evading questions guiltily, Fayiz longed for his Peri wife and made to go back. His first wife, however, said that if he left without explanation she'd abandon their sons to poverty.

Out of fear that she'd leave or harm them he confessed everything and, for the second time, broke a marriage vow. Before he finished speaking, the voice of the invisible Peri sounding much more majestic than she'd ever sounded before thundered: 'Faithless human! My curse upon you: you will never see me or your sons again and shall always be wanting!'

So because he broke his vow to his Peri wife, Fayiz never saw her again. He also wouldn't go back to his family, but lived in the wilderness hoping to meet the beloved Peri once again but finding not one day of peace.

The Cuelebre of Pena Uruel

Spain

In the mountain of Uruel, near the fortified town of Jaca, there lived a dragon or, as the locals it terrorized called it, a *cuelebre.* It was a giant green serpent with enormous wings, sharp claws, and even sharper teeth. This was, to say the least, of a fiery nature— it used its incendiary breath to threaten the villagers and poor peasants into giving it all their livestock to eat and, when that ran out, started asking for the young children (those, it said, tasted best).

Everyone in the vicinity was horrified, but no one

was daring enough to do anything about it. You see, there was something about this dragon that made it seemingly impossible to defeat: its gaze, besides being quite frightful in itself (as dragon teeth are very close to dragon eyes), was deadly. One glance and you're turned to stone! It is, then, understandable that no man nor valiant knight was brave enough to face the beast.

The devastation continued. That is, until one particular morning in which a young lad rode up to the mountain carrying a tin shield, and told everyone who would listen that he was going to take down the cuelebre. The villagers laughed— this boy was not known for his strength and, though very clever, they did not believe he could outmatch a dragon.

He smiled and said nothing, using what time he had before the dragon came to polish his flimsy tin shield so it shone like the sun. And the dragon came slithering down, not bothering to use its wings (it was nice and fat), making the ground shake.

The boy got ready— he didn't even have a sword!— and, when the monster was close, shouted a challenge and hid behind the tin shield. Lo and behold! Though it was no weapon, the shield was just polished enough that it reflected the deadly glare back at the cuelebre, killing it instantly! They were now safe and free!

Amidst disbelieving relief, the villagers carried the boy—now a hero— on their shoulders to the fortified town of Jaca, where he ate to his heart's content and did not have to go hungry ever again.

The Spirit Queen

Indonesia

In a rich kingdom of a wealthy, green island surrounded by warm, plenteous coral reefs and waters, there lived an elderly king and his beautiful, kind daughter, Dewi Kadita. She was his only child by his beloved, late wife, and, as he knew she was wise as well as fair, he wished to leave the throne to her.

Alas, the laws of the kingdom were strict: no woman could inherit the throne. Try as he might, the king could not succeed in altering them in time. So, with a heavy heart full of foreboding, he married again.

His new wife was, indeed, very beautiful — almost as beautiful as Dewi Kadita! However her heart was rotten with pride and jealousy. She hated the princess and wanted her to leave from the first day she stepped foot in the palace. But the old king, enamoured with his deceitful, young wife, saw none of this.

Soon enough the stepmother got with child, and all the wise men and soothsayers predicted it would be a boy. The future king. The elderly sovereign still loved his daughter, though, and still wanted to make her Queen after him. Seeing this, the stepmother was even more jealous, and her will grew poisonous. She would see this vain princess sent away.

With wiles and threats, she pestered the king. Day and night, she complained about his daughter. Of course, her husband knew Dewi Kadita had done nothing wrong, and so he did not punish her. But he was weary. And so, one day he told his new wife, 'I shall not disown my daughter. If you want her to go away, arrange so yourself,' and, thinking she would not dare, he spoke no more of it.

The stepmother saw her chance. With a few chosen servants she traveled deep into the jungle, to the hut of an old, dark witch with a heart, she thought, as venomous as herself. There, she requested a spell to banish the princess. 'Put this in her drinking water,' the old woman said, 'and watch the spell work.' But the witch took pity on the good princess (even she knew how kind she was), when the Queen wasn't looking, she added another enchantment to the powder.

The king's wife did as she was told and, soon enough, the princess fell very ill. She would not leave her bedchamber, nor let anyone see her. A servant, however, peeked into her room and, horrified, went to the king's council with a horrifying tale. The once beautiful princess had been changed into a terrible monster with sagging, falling, blistering skin. He'd never seen anything like it!

It was true. The council, the king and his wife (with a dark satisfaction in her soul), saw it. Despite the old sovereign's pleas for mercy, the nobles decided: it was needful to banish the daughter.

No longer a princess, Dewi Kadita was cast out. She wandered far and wide looking for a place to rest, but whoever saw her would chase her away. No one recognised her. No one helped her.

One night, after she had found some fruit and a tree root for shelter, a veiled figure appeared to her. She didn't know it, but it was the witch who had given her stepmother the awful spell. Now, the old woman had come to complete the other part of the enchantment. She approached the frightened girl.

'Dewi Kadita,' she whispered, 'You have been cast out and treated unfairly. I will help you know.' And she gave her precise instructions on what to do: 'Go to the sea.

Stand on the cliff close to the palace grounds and jump into the water. Trust me. Make sure no one sees you.' And, just as she came, the old woman was gone.

Full of doubts but with renewed hope, the still kindly and good Dewi Kadita journeyed back to the sea. She traveled by night. After many days of fitful sleep and many moons of despair, she arrived. The cliff was taller than she remembered. Could she do it? Would she jump?

The old woman's words filled her heart. She wanted to be well again. She wanted to see her beloved father again, and her dear palace companions. Soaring with courage and determination, she took the plunge. It seemed to her like a very long time but, finally, she felt the warm water enveloping her aching body.

She could not swim. The waves were harsh. Dewi Kadita felt herself sink deeper and deeper, hopelessly.

All of a sudden, the old witch's hidden enchantment came alive: the water became less punishing. Small fish surrounded the princess with many-coloured fins. Dancing porpoises hung flowering seaweed around her neck. The waves lapped at her skin, cleansing it of all impurity. It seemed like an age of the world.

Finally, the surface broke. The nobles and fishermen who were near saw an unparalleled radiance rising from the water. With shielded eyes, they glanced at the source. It was a maiden, glowing with beauty, iridescent fish scales covering her lower limbs. A mermaid had been born — and more than a mermaid. Everyone recognised the features of the good banished princess.

The king and his court, flustered by the news, hurried to the shore. What they saw was no longer a human maiden but a being as glorious and delicate as the sunlight filtered through coral reefs. Dewi Kadita had become Nyi Roro Kidul, the sovereign of the seas.

Because of her goodness and her virtue she had accomplished something no one expected: she was immortal, lovely, and the Queen of her very own realm: the Kingdom of the Southern Seas. She lives through the ages, taking royal husbands as she pleases, reigning with fairness and compassion, and offering good counsel to anyone who seeks the Spirit Queen of the Sea with a clean heart.

Aziza and the Hunter

Benin (Dahomey)

In the beginning the world was wild, unexplored and without medicine. When people got sick, they would slowly waste away and their loved ones could not help them. It was a perilous world.

Even so, there were those who hunted. As there was nothing to cure you if you got hurt, this was an extremely dangerous job. One of these hunters — a very daring one — had a beloved wife who was a leper. He was the bravest, truest, most compassionate soul to walk the earth. But, still, he could not help she who he loved the most.

One morning as he was walking in the woods waiting for his prey to show up, he heard a small voice coming from a mound of earth. It said, 'Hunter, I have something to cure your wife. I am Aziza, the Lord of the Forest.' Aziza ordered the hunter to turn around and, when he did so, he said, 'I give you this bounty of leaves, this medicine of earth. Take them, pound them then mix them with water. Your wife will drink them, and be healed'.

The hunter went back to the village and did exactly as he was told. The next day, his wife was completely cured and well! He cried for joy and went back into the perilous jungle to thank the Aziza. The voice ordered him to send all the sick people in the village to him, so that they would be cured.

Over time, the fame of the village grew: everyone knew that whoever was sick and went there came back a new man. When the rumours reached the King, he travelled to the forest with a majestic entourage. He toiled through the jungle and arrived at the mound with plentiful gifts of rum and palm oil and, when the Aziza's voice greeted him, said 'We have no vodun (meaning gods). Come to our Kingdom and heal us, and be our god'.

That day the powerful Aziza left the mound and went with the King, for there was much good to be done. This fair spirit healed the entire Kingdom, blessed the crops and taught many about medicine and the sacredness of nature. He showed them how to worship the real gods so they would become a rich and happy people. And, over everything else, he taught them to value the Earth and the medicine gifts it provides.

The Seven-Headed Manitou

Canada (Ojibwe)

On a farm, there lived a poor man with his wife. They had no children. One day, desperate for food, the man went fishing and caught a very slippery trout. The animal said to him, 'Wait! I'll grant you a gift: do not throw away any of my scales, but bury them in your garden. Give your wife half of my body to eat, and the other half to the dog.' Of course, the man obeyed the talking fish. He told his wife about the strange instructions he'd received, and they did as they were told.

Can you imagine the surprise of these poor farmers

when, by the next morning, all their animals, plants, and money had been doubled? They were not poor anymore! That night, the wife conceived and, as they found out nine moons later, they had a pair of healthy, strapping twins.

As they now had everything they needed, no one in the family went outside the bounds of their land. But, as growing lads are always curious, one of the twins asked their father, 'Are there other people in the world?'. 'Of course!' replied the father and realised, only too late, that this son would leave them and go travel to make his own fortune.

With tears, they let him go. He took with him the dog (who had eaten half of the fish body and was now magical), and they walked for days before finding anyone at all. But, finally, he saw a town all decked in black. It was deathly silent.

He approached the local blacksmith and asked why the town was mourning, and could he stay the night? 'Of course,' the man replied, 'And we are in mourning because all of our maidens have been devoured by the dragon *Manitou* who lives on the mountain, the dreadful Windigo. And, now that no others are left, even the beautiful chief's daughter will have to be sacrificed tomorrow'.

The young man pondered this and, as soon as the sun rose, set out for the mountain. He had, after all, nothing to lose. He was almost there when he saw a beautiful girl weeping, and an old marshal consoling her halfheartedly.

'What's wrong?' the lad asked. 'I'm being taken to the mountain to be eaten by the Windigo,' she replied sadly. 'It cannot be helped!' the marshal added, 'It's for the common good.'

The hero thought him cold and, with bravery in his voice, instructed the girl to stay put: he would deal with the Windigo himself. With a glimpse of hope in her lovely eyes, the chief's daughter gave him a ring and wished him luck.

Taking heart, he climbed the steep slopes and, when he reached the top, waited. Suddenly, he felt the earth tremble and the trees around him shake. The air grew hot, dense, and poisonous: the Manitou had arrived. With a roar, it appeared.

The monster one powerful, armored body and seven ghastly heads that thrashed, looking for a maiden to bite and devour. When the fourteen awful eyes found him and realised he was no the morsel they were expecting, the Windigo attacked.

The hero dashed this way and that, struggling to avoid the Manitou's many sharp fangs and claws until, finally, he cut one of the heads off. It grew again! Suddenly realizing what he had to do, the young man cut it off again and tossed it to his dog, telling him to hold onto it. With a great deal of effort, he managed to do the same with the remaining heads and, at last, the Manitou lay dead atop the mountain.

After cutting off the seven tongues of the dragon as a trophy and a gift for the girl's father, the lad descended to where the chief's daughter and the marshal waited and gave her the tongues.

Our hero was exhausted and, though he thought of resting on the ground for a little while, he fell into a deep sleep. The girl thought there was no harm in coming down without him— she would go first and announce him to his father.

But, on the way back, the old, cowardly marshal said, 'You will give me the tongues and tell your father it was I who killed the Manitou. If you refuse, I will kill you.' Afraid, the girl did as she was told and her father, pleased to see his daughter again, announced she and the marshal were to be married that very night— even though she did not want to.

When the wedding feast was going on, the hero—finally awake— walked in and immediately understood what had happened. When the girl saw him, she took her chance and told her father the truth of what had happened. 'He has my ring as proof that this is true,' she explained.

Ashamed to have been played for a fool, the chief walked up to the hero, who was sitting near the door and invited him to a place of honour. When the traitorous marshal saw this, he tried to escape but was caught. The chief declared him guilty and, with great applause from the crowd, he was thrown out onto the stormy sea in a little barge.

The hero, however, received great honour and married the chief's daughter who loved him, as he had saved her at his own risk. They were happy for many years and became powerful, prosperous, and famous.

The Goodman O'Wastness

Orkney Islands

In Wastness, a small fishing village, there lived a man. Alone. His friends, family, and neighbours wondered why he would not take a wife. Every time they asked, he just smiled and shook his head. He knew they thought that he ought to marry, and he knew that he was rich, smart, and good enough (so good, in fact, that the village called him 'Goodman'!). He never said a word about it.

But, within his heart, he knew why he would not take a wife. He was of the mind that women were all evil — all mean and quarrelsome and vain. A petty opinion, if you ask me, and one he would grow to regret.

Goodman O'Wastness looked the other way when the loveliest village girls turned to stare at him. If they talked to him, he would only reply 'Yes' and 'No', which frustrated them to no end. Since he was so aloof and alone, they felt they wanted to marry him and make him smile. But none of them was fated to do so, and Goodman O'Wastness went about his merry, lonely way.

One day, after going out to sea to fish, he was pulling his small boat out onto the sand for the night — and he saw them.

Creatures more beautiful than the human mind can fathom were lying in the shallow water, sunning themselves in the last rays of the day. Then, when he finally could draw his eyes away from their mysterious beauty, he saw something else. Something very curious.

Seal skins. They were selkies! He should have known! If you are as lost as our hero used to be, know this: selkies are shape-shifting creatures. When they are in the water, which is their home, they look just like other seals. But they retain the ability to take off their seal skins whenever they wish to, and to turn into the most graceful, radiant maidens your eyes ever did see.

Now, Goodman O'Wastness knew what he would do. His heart had been, against his better judgement, captured. He would capture a seal skin in exchange.

The shapeshifting power of selkies — all their magic — lies in their skins. Take those away and they are simple, powerless humans like you and me. Well, almost. The heart remains a selkie heart.

The man approached in silence, with careful stealth. When he was close enough, he snatched a skin and held it to his chest. At once, cries of horror sprang all about, and selkies rushed to find their own sea gowns. After the commotion died down, there was only one weeping maiden left. 'Please,' she begged, 'Give me back my skin! I cannot live on land!' But Goodman was silent and walked home, leaving the maiden no choice but to follow.

Once they arrived, he locked the magical seal skin in a secure wooden chest and hid the key on the roofbeams over the bed. The maiden saw none of this.

Days and weeks passed. The selkie kept crying, but she had no choice but to remain. Goodman O'Wastness, however, felt a new thing budding in his heart. It was love. He brought the fair maiden the best fish, the nicest human clothes, and was as kind to her as any lover has ever been. After some time she began to warm up to his advances, and eventually promised to remain with him as his human wife, even though she had been married to a selkie man in the sea.

The Selkie Wife stayed for three years with Goodman O'Wastness. In that time they had three children that were as beautiful as their mother — but wholly human.

After those three years, the girl began to feel a deep longing in her heart. It had never truly left — that need to be in the sea —, but now it was stronger than ever. She searched high and low for the key to her seal skin. All to no avail.

One day she could no longer take it and started weeping just as miserably as the first day, when Goodman had taken her magical skin for the first time. 'Mama, what's wrong?' her youngest child asked and, upon hearing what she was looking for, exclaimed, 'I know! Yesterday, Papa climbed on the bed and took a key from the roof beams to glower at it!'

With wild happiness beating in her chest, the Selkie Wife reached for the key, opened the lock and, after three long, heavy years, was reunited with her seal skin. She hugged her three children and headed for the sea, to be reunited with her selkie husband and dance in the waves for the rest of her life. Goodman O'Wastness never saw her, nor any other selkie, ever again.

If you love something, do not try to keep it for yourself. If you must, let it go and be content with the beauty and joy that seeing it brings.

The Tale of Rowli Pugh

Wales

There was once a small, charming village in South Wales in the area called Glamorganshire. The villagers were hard-working, normal people who devoted their days to mining, farming, ploughing and getting fatter and more prosperous. There was nothing extraordinary about them.

Despite the general abundance, not everyone shared in the good luck. On the outskirts of the village there was a small, rundown farmstead. That was the house of poor Rowli Pugh and his sick wife, Catti Jones.

Rowli Pugh was as kind a fellow as you could wish to meet, and everyone knew he had a good heart. After all hadn't he married that frail, sickly woman out of sheer love? However, they couldn't but hold his poverty against him. At first when the couple started having trouble finding food for the biting wintertime, the villagers helped them. But, soon enough, they became tired of lending a hand. 'I have my own family,' they said, 'They brought this poverty on themselves'. Everyone knew it: Rowli Pugh was unlucky. So no one helped anymore.

Day by day the couple's pantry dwindled, while the cold weather still seemed to stay. Catti Jones had no strength to cook, sew and help with the farm work like other wives. Rowli Pugh loved her dearly, but he went without food all too often. His heart was low and both his animal pens and his pockets were empty. The roof leaked. There was nothing growing in the vegetable garden. He knew that if nothing changed his wife would die from the cold and the illness, and that he, heartbroken, would soon follow her.

On that particular day, they'd eaten the last of their grain. The last chicken had been stolen. The house wall had fallen down. Defeated and hearing his tired, beloved wife coughing in the cold house, our hero slumped by the wall, lamenting his evil luck in the winter sunlight.

Then, he felt it: someone was watching him. Lifting his head, Rowli Pugh saw a tiny man dressed in funny, colourful clothing. It was an ellyll — an elf! The ellyll asked him what the matter was and, before poor, speechless Rowli Pugh could reply, he spoke again.

'There, there. Don't say a word. I know more about your heart than anyone — even you! We've seen your goodness and know you married this girl out of love. It's time we turned your luck around!' He instructed Rowli only to ask his wife to leave a burning candle out when going to bed, and to never, ever peek into the kitchen at night.

Catti Jones did as her husband asked. Every night, she swept the modest kitchen and left a burning candle out. Every morning they were amazed: there was rich food on the table, everything was clean, Rowli's working clothes were mended and half their work was already done!

Rowli, well fed and clean, started to work harder and got money for his efforts. He invested the money on better land and good, sturdy animals. Even Catti's health miraculously improved! By springtime, they were a completely changed couple — they were even well-off.

But one night, Catti could no longer avoid her curiosity: who was doing the work for them? She wanted to thank them, wanted to see. After Rowli was asleep, she sneaked out and peeked into the kitchen. There, dancing and singing, jumping and cavorting was a family of minuscule ellyll! They laughed and joked and twirled while they worked. Unable to hold in her amusement at these strange merrymakers, Catti joined in the laughter.

Everything stopped. Silence. They were gone. In the morning, Catti told her husband about her mistake. He forgave her — after all, they were rich now. They were healthy and could work hard: they didn't need the elves' good luck any longer. Neither of them saw the ellyll again, but everyone marvelled at their change in fortune and newfound happiness. And, as thanks, Rowli Pugh left some milk and bread out, with a candle, every winter night.

The Dragon Princess

China

In the Sea of Dungting, in the East there are a great many wondrous and mysterious things, and, among them, a bottomless hole. So what happened when a distracted, dirty, and lost fisherman fell in?

When he fell into the hole, he kept falling for a long time. But, eventually, he arrived at a country with green, rolling hills as well as very odd plants and animals he'd never before seen. Walking in amazement, he found himself before a great castle and directly in front of the snout of an enormous sea dragon. Wrinkling its face in distaste, the creature merely refused him entry but didn't harm him.

After some time of exploration, he found a way out and went directly to the Emperor. He told the court everything about this strange new land. The Emperor's wise man became very excited: he knew many things about the Dragon People of the Dungting Sea. For example, that they hated tree wax (the fisherman's clothes reeked of it, and so the dragons hadn't touched him). More importantly, he knew that every dragon has, at least, one magical pearl that it keeps under his chin.

But the Sea King's daughter, the Dragon Princess, whose castle the fisherman had seen, had a whole hoard of them tucked away. The wise man proposed that the Emperor should send his most courteous and worthy messengers, armed with a protective stone, to see the Dragon Princess. They would take a load of swallows (the Dragons' favourite meal) and dragon-brain vapour, which would compel their hosts to give them the treasure they sought.

Lo-Dsi-Tschun and his two brothers were chosen as envoys, as they were related to the Dragon King through a distant ancestor. After being wholly dunked in smelly tree wax (just a precaution, as dragons are always perilous), the brothers set out. They offered swallows to the guards, who devoured the food and, disliking the smell of the brothers, let them pass.

When they arrived at the castle, they were received by the Dragon Princess and her own wise counselor, a thousand-year-old dragon who could turn into a human at will. He read the letter from the Emperor, which demanded a gift of magical pearls in exchange for a thousand delicious swallows.

The Princess smiled enigmatically. The brothers were treated courteously: they got the best fare of their lives— all flowers and fine herbs— and couldn't resist sneaking some into their saddlebags for the way home.

Eventually, thanks to the offerings done to her, the Princess consented, just for once, to give the Emperor the magical pearls he sought: a total of ten supernatural ones and innumerable common ones. The brothers, grateful not to have been eaten, bowed low. Their amazement was even greater when they were invited to ride to the surface on the back of a twisting, dancing dragon. They were sure that half the turns he took were only intended to make them feel dizzy and lost. Dragons like that sort of jokes.

Back at the court, the brothers handed the treasure to the Emperor and the whole court admired it, as well as their bravery and negotiating skills.

As for Lo-Dsi-Tschun and the other two travellers, they opened the bags to eat the rest of the marvelous food they had brought back only to discover that, in contact with the harsh air of our reality, it had become as hard as a stone!

The three brothers laughed and looked at each other with a light in their hearts. It did not matter that they got no prize for their dangerous journey. Sometimes, they had learnt, an adventure in which you meet creatures far greater than you knew before is, in itself, its own reward.

Made in the USA
Las Vegas, NV
03 January 2024

83826503R00066